MW01255884

Japji Sahib
The Song of the Soul

Guru Nanak

Translated by

Ek Ong Kaar Kaur Khalsa

Perfect Publications

To order additional copies of this book, contact:
Xlibris Corporation
1-888-795-4274
www.Xlibris.com
Orders@Xlibris.com
26762

Thank you to:

My mother and father who gave me life.

All the teachers I have had along the way.

The Guru who brought me
To the feet of the Siri Singh Sahib
Who, in turn,
Brought me to the feet of the Guru.

Acknowledgement

If one is very fortunate in life, a person may have the touch of a living Master. It was by amazing grace that, as I wandered lost, searching for a path to take me out of the pain of modern life, the Creator brought me to the feet of the Siri Singh Sahib Bhai Sahib Harbhajan Singh Khalsa Yogiji.

As both a Sikh and a Master of Kundalini Yoga, the Siri Singh Sahib, also known as Yogi Bhajan, teaches a powerful Dharma. It is a Dharma for the householder—where through the Sikh spiritual practice of the Shabd Guru—the Guru as Divinely Given Sound—supported with the practice of Kundalini Yoga, one can live in balance with the heavens and the earth, seeing the Divine Light in everything while being an active, social, healthy, happy and holy human being.

Japji Sahib was written by the first of the Sikh Gurus, Guru Nanak, at the turn of the 16th century. It was under the Siri Singh Sahib's guidance and direction that this translation of Japji Sahib, was undertaken. There are so many stories to tell about the process of translating Japji Sahib. But the key was his faith in me and his insistence that I go past my self imposed limits as a person and a writer.

It is with tremendous love, affection and a deep deep gratitude that I dedicate this translation to him. He left his physical body on October 6, 2004. All knew him as a rare and amazing spirit who had a unique courage, giving people a chance to face their deepest fears, their darkest demons and come through the experience victorious and triumphant.

No project is ever individual and nothing happens in isolation. There were countless other people who, by God's grace, gave their time, love, devotion and assistance in the completion of this translation.

Dr. Balkar Singh, the Director of the GRD Institute of Language and Culture in Espanola, New Mexico and the former head of the Siri Guru Granth Sahib Department at Punjabi University in Patiala, India spent months going over

Japji Sahib with me line by line, word by word. I am grateful for all that he taught me and for the great dialogue on Sikh tradition and thought that such an in-depth study of Japji provoked.

Dr. Bibiji Inderjit Kaur, the Bhai Sahiba of Sikh Dharma International and the wife of the Siri Singh Sahib, was so very supportive of the translation process. Her love, encouragement and insights were tremendously helpful and a very precious gift.

MSS Shakti Parwha Kaur Khalsa, the Mother of 3HO, took the time to read through the translation and share her wisdom, insights, and edits. She has been a sounding board for everything I have written about Sikh Dharma, and her frank, humorous guidance has been a saving grace.

MSS Guruka Singh Khalsa, who has also translated Japji, has been a confidant and an invaluable part of the editing process, as well. SS Dev Suroop Kaur Khalsa has been my comrade-at-arms through this project, sharing every moment of frustration and joy as the process of translating Japji deeply transformed my own life. Joginder Singh and Joginder Kaur Manchanada and their son Supreet Singh shared valuable perspectives on Japji from the point of view of Sikh history, culture and tradition that were tremendously helpful in understanding the text.

There were countless others, too numerous to name, who gave their prayers, encouragement, time and support along the way. I would especially like to thank my sister Michelle Martin and my friends Pavitar Kaur (Windsong), Sampuran Singh Khalsa and Jagat Joti Singh Khalsa for their love and support in making the publishing of this translation a reality and for believing in the relevance and importance of this project with far more heart and love than I could ever have hoped.

Last, but not least, I would to thank my father and mother, James and Dee Gillece, who gave me life, provided me an excellent education and always told me that I could do whatever I put my mind to. Mom and Dad, I love you.

Through Guru Nanak, may Thy Spirit forever increase and may all people prosper by Thy grace. Naanak Naam, Charhdee Kalaa, Tayray Bhaanay Sarbatt Daa Bhalaa. Wahe Guru Ji Ka Khalsa, Wahe Guru Ji Ki Fateh.

Sardarni Sahiba Ek Ong Kaar Kaur Khalsa

Preface

We are walking step by step into the Age of Aquarius where our spiritual identity shall be the primary value and our common humanity the base. Over 500 years ago, Guru Nanak laid down the path when he was given the Divine Song of Japji Sahib. Japji Sahib is 40 steps that give us an understanding of the Total Comprehensive Reality of the Divine and lead us to living in the flow of our own Infinity as humble human householders on the earth.

Guru Nanak recognized that humans had made the whole issue of spirituality too complicated and he sought to simplify it. God is within you and you have the right to experience that happiness, that bliss while living on the earth—no matter what your circumstances in life. It is an awareness, a direct perception, a consciousness that cannot be bought and cannot be sold. But in truly and humbly meditating upon the Words of those who have understood this truth, the same truth can be awakened within you.

Guru Nanak, along with his musician companion Mardana, traveled far and wide in the late 15th and early 16th centuries through what is now northern India, Pakistan, Tibet, and Southeast Asia—always on foot. He brought together people of different religions and different social classes to sit together, in love, and sing meditative songs of the Creator and the greatness of life. Guru Nanak was a pioneer and a revolutionary—tearing down the walls of prejudice against women 500 years ago. He saw the Divine Light of the Creator equally in men and women and established a path where women were held in the highest honor.

Though his physical footsteps are no longer with us, the songs of Guru Nanak and his successors offer us a chance to open ourselves to the love and beauty of life. To the gift of being here, for a time, with each other, sharing and celebrating in the wonder of God's Creation.

The Sacred Way of the Sikhs began with Guru Nanak as a universal path of acceptance, wisdom and love. Through Guru Nanak and the nine succeeding Sikh Gurus, the Shabad Guru came into being—the Divine Teacher and Guide in the form of Sound. Japji Sahib is originally written in the language of Gurmukhi, which literally means *from the Mouth of the Guru*. Even if one does not understand that Divine Language, its Sound Current has the power to profoundly impact our psyche and consciousness, clearing blocks that keep us from experiencing our limitless potential. Awakening our spirit and true destiny.

This English rendition of Japji Sahib is like the moon to the sun. It is only a tiny reflection of the Divine Beauty of the original. If there is something in this that touches your soul, that fires your devotion and love, listen to Japji Sahib in its original form—in the Sound Current of Gurmukhi—and allow yourself to be transformed. The age of mindless suffering is coming to an end. Now is the time to touch that subtlety of existence, which gives us the sophisticated sense that God is here with us, now, in every living thing and that God is love, is peace, and is purposeful.

May you be blessed to live to your Infinity and be with those who live in that same grace, vastness and Light.

Mool Mantra

One Spirit Beyond
Moves within the Creation—
Coordinating
Consolidating
Continually
Creating,

And this Spirit
Within me
Is my True Identity.

It Does All
And Causes All
To be Done.

It Protects me
Through all incidents
Of Time and Space.

It fears nothing
And knows nothing
Of vengeance
Or anger.

Deathless
It comes into Form.

In Itself, It has
Never been born.

Flowing through the cycles
Of Birth and Death,
It moves
By Its Own
Purity and Projection.

This understanding
Shall come to you
As a sweet blessing,
As a gift.

In every moment
Continue
In Its Continual
Remembrance.

From the start
This Truth was True.

All through Time and Space
Is True.

Even now,
This Truth is True.

Nanak says,
Ever shall be True.

1

You think and think
Ten-thousand thoughts,
But not one thought
Will give you
What you seek.

You sit in silence
To find the silence
But silence never comes.
Your spirit always sings
The song of the Divine.

And all your troubles,
And all your cares,
These will never fade away
Though you may hoard
Every treasure in the world.

And all the clever tricks
You use,
The countless little tricks—
Not even one
Will go along with you.

How can we find
The House of Truth?

How can we break
This wall of lies?

Surrender yourself
And walk the Way
Of Spirit's Will.

Nanak,
Be with what
Is already written.

2

Through Spirit's Will
Come countless forms,

Though of this Will
I cannot speak.

Through Spirit's Will
Come all the souls.

Merge in that Will
And become great.

In Spirit's Will
Are good and bad.

That Will writes
Pain and peace
For all.

For some, it brings
Abundant gifts.

For some, it leads
To endless wanderings.

Everything exists within that Will.
Nothing lies
Beyond It.

Nanak,
If you understand
The Will of the Divine,
Your ego will have
Nothing to say.

3

When the soul
Tunes in
To the Infinite

And spontaneously sings
With Divine love and joy,

In that soul-singing,
Some capture Your power.

But who has the power
To capture Your power?

When the soul
Tunes in
To the Infinite

And spontaneously sings
With Divine love and joy,

In that soul-singing
Some sing of You
As a Giver
And know giving
As the sign of You.

When the soul
Tunes in
To the Infinite

And spontaneously sings
With Divine love and joy,

In that soul-singing
Some sing of
Your virtues,
The elements You use
To create life,
And how amazing
It all is.
How magnificently beautiful.

When the soul
Tunes in
To the Infinite

And spontaneously sings
With Divine love and joy,

In that soul-singing
Some sing
Of the knowledge
That can only be gotten
By arduous study.

When the soul
Tunes in
To the Infinite

And spontaneously sings
With Divine love and joy,

In that soul-singing
Some sing
Of the Power that
Creates all things
Sustains them
And destroys them.

When the soul
Tunes in
To the Infinite

And spontaneously sings
With Divine love and joy,

In that soul-singing
Some sing
Of how You
Take the souls away
And then
Give them back again.

When the soul
Tunes in
To the Infinite,

And spontaneously sings
With Divine love and joy

In that soul-singing,
Some sing
Of how far beyond
Our reach, our grasp
You are.

When the soul
Tunes in
To the Infinite

And spontaneously sings
With Divine love and joy,

In that soul-singing
Some sing
You are always with us.

There is no end
To what
We can say
About You.

Millions of people
Speak
Millions of ways.

You, Great Giver,
Keep giving to us
And we grow tired
Of just taking.

Age after age
You continually
Feed and
Nourish us.

In Your Will,
Oh Divine Spirit,
You guide us along
The path You choose for us.

Nanak,
Blissful,
Hasn't a care.

4

True is the Master
Of Creation.

True is His Spirit
Within me.

Speak it with Infinite Love.

We call on You
And beg to You,
"Give me, give me."

And you, Great Giver,
Give it All.

What can we
Place before You
That will allow us
To see the splendor
Of Your Divine and Noble Court?

What words can we speak
With our own lips
That, upon hearing,
You would touch us
With Your Love?

In the Amrit Veyla,
The still hours before sunrise,
Our True Spirit
Becomes known
As we meditate upon
Your Greatness.

By the consequences
Of our positive past actions,
We have been gifted
This robe of human form.

Grace leads us
To the gate of liberation
Found within it.

Nanak,
In this way know,
All people
Hold the Truth
Within themselves.

5

Nothing has
Established You
Or placed You
On Your throne.

Neither are You
Created by anything.

You within Yourself
Are pure
Like the crystal
Cool, clear water
Of a stream.

Those who serve You,
You bestow upon them
So much honor.

Nanak sings
Of Your virtues,
Your priceless gifts and treasures.

Sing.
Deeply listen.
And oh my mind
Overflow with Love.

All suffering shall vanish,
And peace,
Sweet peace,
Shall make its home
In your heart.

The wise person
Who flows
With the integrity
Of the Guru's words
Is one
With the Naad,
The subtle vibration
Which powers creation.

The wise person
Who flows
With the integrity
Of the Guru's words
Is one
With all scriptures written
And yet to be written.

The wise person
Who flows
With the integrity
Of the Guru's words
Remains continually
Within herself
With Thee.

The Guru,
The Divine Teacher,
Can take the form
Of Shiva.

That Guru
Can take the form
Of Vishnu or Brahma.

That Divine Teacher
Can even take the form
Of the Divine Mother.

Even if I know all this,
Still there's no way
To speak it,
No matter how much I say.

The Divine Teacher
Has given me
One lesson to learn.

All souls come
From the hand of One Giver.

May I never, ever
Forget Him.

6

I wash myself
In sacred waters
In order to please You.

But if it doesn't please You,
What is the bathing for?

I see
The vastness of Your wondrous creation.

But without taking action,
How can I merge with Thee?

Within my own
Awareness
Are jewels, gems
And rubies,
From listening to the Teachings
Of the Guru
Even once.

All souls come
From the Hand of One Giver.

May I never, ever
Forget Him.

7

If a person were to live
Through the four ages
Or ten times that,

Known across
The nine continents
Followed by everyone.

Protected by a good name,
With fame and reputation
Received from the entire world.

Yet, if You do not look kindly
Our way, oh Divine One,
That position
Nobody would want.
Such a one would be
The worm
That lives inside worms.

Among criminals—
The most criminal.

Nanak,
The virtueless and the virtuous
Are both created by the Divine.

And what virtues they carry
Are given by Thee.

No one exists
Who can bestow virtues on You.

8

Those who are merged in You,
Those who spiritually lead,
Angels,
Masters
Deeply Listen.

The Earth,
And what holds the Earth,
And what surrounds the Earth
Inter-coordinate
By Deep Listening.

The Continents,
Other Realms,
Lower Worlds,
Work together
By Deep Listening.

Deeply Listening,
Death
Cannot touch you.

Nanak,
Those who surrender themselves in Love
To the Divine
Continually blossom and bloom.

Deeply Listening,
Sorrows
And errors
Depart.

9

Deeply Listening,
The Three Aspects
Of the Divine—
Generator
Organizer
Deliverer/Destroyer
Maintain their balance
And dance.

Deeply Listening,
Even those
With an imbalanced mind
Praise Thee
With their lips.

Deeply Listening,
Yoga
And the hidden systems
Of the body
Make themselves known.

Deeply Listening,
The wisdom
Of all sacred scriptures in the world
Is revealed.

Nanak,
Those who surrender themselves in Love
To the Divine
Continually blossom and bloom.

Deeply Listening,
Sorrows
And errors
Depart.

10

Deeply Listening,
Truth,
Complete, utter contentment
And genuine wisdom
Will be with you
Within you.

Deeply Listening,
The purity
From bathing
In all sacred waters
Will cleanse you.

Deeply Listening,
The same honor comes
As if you had continually
Read and studied.

Deeply Listening
Brings you
To the point
Of One-Pointedness,
Flowing with the continual flow
Of the Divine Spirit
In meditative delight.

Nanak,
Those who surrender themselves in Love
To the Divine
Continually blossom and bloom.

Deeply Listening,
Sorrows
And errors
Depart.

11

Deeply Listening,
Recognize
The ocean of virtues
Within you.

Deeply Listening
Become
In tune with Spirit,
Perfectly balanced
In your own humanity
And nobility.

Deeply Listening,
Even blind
You will find your way.

Deeply Listening,
Understand
The unfathomable.

Nanak,
Those who surrender themselves in Love
To the Divine
Continually blossom and bloom.

Deeply Listening,
Sorrows
And errors
Depart.

12

Trust what you hear
When you listen—
Even though
You won't be able
To explain it
To anyone,

And even if you do
Talk about it,
You'll just regret it
Afterwards.

There is no person
Who, with their pen,
Has the power to describe
All that is heard
When you deeply listen.

Those who sit together
And trust what they hear
When they listen
Are doing
The most powerful
Meditation.

Such is
That True Spirit
Within me
That it makes me become
Pure, clear and sweet.

If you
Trust what you hear
When you listen,
That knowing
Becomes the psyche
Through which you
Reflect, understand
And act.

13

By trusting
What you hear
When you listen,
The Truth
Of your own Inner
Consciousness
Will saturate your psyche
With wisdom
And deep understanding.

By trusting
What you hear
When you listen,
You shall dwell
In all mansions
Of learning.

In trusting
What you hear
When you listen,
The blows and insults
Of others
Will not affect you.

By trusting
What you hear
When you listen,
Death will have
No power over you.

Such is
That True Spirit
Within me
That it makes me become
Pure, clear and sweet.

If you
Trust what you hear
When you listen,
Then you will know
What you see,
How to understand
And act.

14

In trusting
What you hear
When you listen,
There will be
No obstacles
On your path.

In trusting
What you hear
When you listen,
Radiance and honor
Will be with you.

In trusting
What you hear
When you listen,
There'll be no need
To take short-cuts
On your journey.

In trusting
What you hear
When you listen,
Dharma,
The path of Divine
Discipline and law,
Will guide
Your whole life.

Such is
That True Spirit
Within me
That it makes me become
Pure, clear and sweet.

If you
Trust what you hear
When you listen,
That knowing
Becomes the psyche
Through which you
Reflect, understand
And act.

15

Trust what you hear
When you listen
And find
The door of liberation.

Trust what you hear
When you listen,
And bring all your loved ones
Along.

Trust what you hear
When you listen.
You will swim across
All difficulties
And your very presence
Will carry others
Across, as well.

And that is what it means
To be a Sikh of the Guru,
A seeker of Divine Wisdom,
Who walks from the darkness of ego
To the light
Of your own purity and spirit.

Trust what you hear
When you listen.
Nanak,
Even if you wander
Lost
There will be no need
To beg for anything.

Such is
That True Spirit
Within me
That it makes me become
Pure, clear and sweet.

If you
Trust what you hear
When you listen,
Then you will know
What you see,
How to understand
And act.

16

Those who,
In the Purity of their own Spirits,
Have recognized
Their essential union with God—
They become the Living Lights
On the earth
To whom all Creation bows.

Holding the Truth of the Divine
Within their very auras,
They become True Leaders
On the earth.

In the Royal Court
Of the Divine
Those who have recognized
Their own purity
Receive the greatest honors.

Standing at the door
Of the Divine, the Supreme and Noble
Leader of leaders,
They are radiant.

The Pure Ones,
Through the Guru
Meditate
On the One.

By doing
The deepest reflection,
Still-The Doer of Doers
Cannot be
Contained
Or comprehended.

Dharma,
The divinely-given
Spiritual law and discipline,
Is the Bull upon which
The entire Universe rests
And is born as the son
Of Mother Compassion.

Deep and continuous patience
Is the mantra
And the thread
Which holds it all in place
And binds everything together.

If someone understands this,
Then that person becomes
The Custodian of Truth.

How much weight
Does the Bull of Divine Law
Carry on its back?

There are so many lands,
Here and beyond.

What power is there
That supports him
And what he carries?

The names,
And the colors
Of all the different souls
Are continuously written
By the same Pen.

If someone were
To try to know Thee
By writing
All that You have
Written

How much
Writing
Would it take?

How many forms are there
Awesome in their power
And beauty?

How many gifts?

Who can know
Their limits?

With one gesture
You, oh Divine One, created
The entire Universe.

From that,
100,000 rivers
Come into being—
Currents that run through,
Nurturing the cycle of life.

What of Your
Universal, Unfathomable
And profoundly Feminine
Creative Power
Can I speak
Or reflect?

I cannot even once
Be a sacrifice to Thee.

What pleases Thee
Is the only good
Worth doing.

Oh Divine Spirit,
You are ever
Indestructible,
Unbound and Beyond Form.

17

Countless are those who call on Thee.
Countless those who Love.
Countless those who do the ceremonies of Fire.
Countless those who purify themselves through their Inner Fire.

Countless the revered and learned ones
Who recite and speak Your sacred words.

Countless those who practice Yoga,
And live detached from their own minds.

Countless those who have surrendered themselves
In love and devotion to Thee,
Gathering virtue, wisdom and deep reflection.

Countless the respectful persons.
Countless the givers.

Countless the heroes who bear the brunt
Of battle.

Countless those who live in silence,
Attuned to Your Divine Song.

What of your
Universal, Unfathomable
And profoundly Feminine
Creative power
Can I speak
Or reflect?

I cannot even once
Be a sacrifice to Thee.

What pleases Thee
Is the only good
Worth doing.

Oh Divine Spirit,
You are ever
Indestructible
Beyond and Unbound by Form.

18

Countless the weak persons
Who cannot stand to see
The horrors of the world.

Countless the thieves
Who make their living
By exploiting others.

Countless those
Who use power
In the service
Of their own egos.

Countless those
Who do not tolerate
What they don't
Understand.

Countless those
Who make so many errors
Even their errors
Breed more errors.

Countless those
Who are so wretched
They spread wretchedness
Wherever they go.

Countless those
Who do not know
The Divine is within them,
And spend their lives
Turning humanity
Against each other.

Countless those
Who never find
Anything good to say
And cloud their minds
With their own negativity.

Nanak,
Of my own weaknesses
I speak and see.

I cannot even once
Be a sacrifice to Thee.

What pleases Thee
Is the only good
Worth doing.

Oh Divine Spirit,
You are ever
Indestructible,
Beyond and Unbound by Form.

19

Countless the spirits
Who come into form.

Countless their enjoyment
Of the experience.

There are so very
Many of them
I cannot know
Them all.

Countless those
Who try to speak
Of these things—
What a weight
They burden
Their own minds with.

From Beyond the Beyond
Comes the Vibration
That lives within
Every creature.

From Beyond the Beyond
Come all the Voices
That honor and praise
This wondrous thing.

From Beyond the Beyond
Comes the definition
Of wisdom,
Sacred writings
And virtue.

From Beyond the Beyond
Comes
All that is written,
All that is spoken
And all
Sacred Sound.

From Beyond the Beyond
Comes the Instructions
Of how to attain
Complete Union with the Divine
And surrender yourself
To the experience.

The One who does
All the writing,
No one can write anything
For Him.

Living in the Purity
Of one's own self-existence,
That is how
The True Spirit comes.

That True Spirit
Is within all things
And creates all things.

Without that True Spirit
Nothing would exist.

What of Your
Universal, Unfathomable
And profoundly Feminine
Creative power
Can I speak
Or reflect?

I cannot even once
Be a sacrifice to Thee.
What pleases Thee
Is the only good worth doing.

Oh Divine Spirit,
You are ever
Indestructible,
Beyond and Unbound by Form.

20

When the hands, the feet,
The whole body
Becomes dirty,
Water
Washes it all away.

When clothes are
Stained with urine,
Soap and water
Removes the stain.

But when
Our own psyches
Are polluted with the dirt
That comes from
The errors and pain
We inflict on others,

Only our True Selves
Can restore us
To our Original Color.

The virtuous,
The unvirtuous,
What a person says
Does not determine
Who he is.

It is the actions we perform
Over and over again
That get recorded
And go along with us.

What seeds I sow,
That food
I have to eat.

Nanak,
In the Will of the Divine,
We come and we go.

21

Sacred baths,
Practices of the Inner Fire,
Kindness,
Giving gifts—
Even if someone
Has the consciousness
To do these things,
It will only bring
A sesame seed's worth
Of honor.

Deeply Listening,
Trusting what you hear when you listen,
Let your mind
Be kindled
In love.

Find the sacred bathing place
Within your own self
And wash off
The filth.

All virtues are Yours, my Beloved.
Of my own,
I have none at all.

And without Your virtues
Devotion to You
Is not even possible.

I am enamored of Thee,
O Primal One—
Beyond Time and Space
Who, through Your Word,
Brings the Creative Forces
Of the Universe into play.

What was that time?
What epoch?
What phase of the moon?
What day of the sun?
What season?
What month?
When the Formless
Took Form?

The spiritual scholars
Have never figured it out,
And they have said as much
In their sacred books.

The season and the day
Is not known
By the Yogis.

The season and the month
Is not known by anyone.

When did the Great Creator
Form the earth
With His Hands?
Only He, Himself,
Knows.

How can i
Find the words?
How can I honor and praise it?
How can I picture it?
How can I even
Know it?

Nanak,
With words,
Everyone talks about it—
Each person
Trying to be
More clever and wise
Than the last.

Great is the Master,
Great is His Spirit within me,
Created by His own Command.

Nanak,
If anybody
Within themselves
Thinks they know You,
There will be nothing for them
When they die.

22

There are worlds and worlds
Below us.

There are worlds and worlds
Above us.

In the end,
In the end
You'll grow tired
Searching them all.

The sacred scriptures
Say this
With one voice.

There are 18,000 worlds,
The scriptures say,
Countless worlds.

But the Source Beyond the Source
Is only One.
Writing this down,
It becomes a written record.

But in time
What is written
Will be destroyed.

Nanak,
What is truly great
Is to know Yourself.

23

Those in a state of joy
Praise Thee.
Yet, in this manner
True Spiritual Understanding
Is not given or received.

Streams and rivers
Flow along,
Not knowing
They are merging
Into the Ocean.

That Ocean
Is the Great, True
Noble Ruler
Who guards the wealth
And jewels
Of spiritual learning.

Even an ant
Is not left behind
If he never forgets God
From his mind.

24

There is no end
To all that You
Create and do.

What we can
Say about You,
There's no end to that, either.

There is no end
To Your actions.

And to what
You give
There is no end.

There is no end
To what we see.

And to what we hear
There is no end.

There is no end
To the visions created
By You coming
Into Form.

There is no end.
The visions go on
As far as we can see.

There is a limit
To our understanding
Of Thee.

How many veils
Like this
Do we have to go through?

There is no end
To Thee, my Beloved.

This is the understanding
I've received
And go along with.

This Unending
Anybody can know.

The more we talk,
The more there is to say.

Great is the Master
In the Highest Place.

Even Higher still
Is His Spirit
Within me.

Any person
Can be
In this height.

And in this height,
You will know God.

How great You are
And how great it is
To know You.

Nanak,
Grace and karma
Are both Thy gifts.

25

There are so many
Karmic plays,
It isn't possible
To write them all.

The Great Giver
Withholds nothing—
Not even the tiniest
Sesame seed.

There are so many warriors
Begging to merge into Thee.
There are so many
Who are counting
But never
Reflect on or see You.

So many are exhausted
Having broken themselves
On vice.

There are so many
Who take everything
And then deny
Receiving.

So many foolish ones
Do nothing but
Stuff their face
With food.

So many are
Continually beaten down
By endless pain and hunger.

Even these
Are your Gifts to us
Great Giver.

Slavery.
Freedom.
Both come
From You.

It isn't possible
For anyone
To say more
Than this.

If someone
Who likes the sound
Of his own voice
Tries to speak
About this,

He'll be shamed
In so many ways.

You, Yourself, know.
You, Yourself, give.

Those who can speak of it
This way
Are very few.

The ones You bless
To meditatively and lovingly
Chant and sing
Your wonders,

Nana
Those persons
Are the nobility
Of nobility.

26

Beyond Price
Are Your virtues.

Beyond Price
Is trading
In Your virtues.

Beyond Price
Are those who live
By trading
In Your virtues.

Beyond Price
Is the store house,
The body,
Where these treasures
Are kept.

Beyond Price
Are those who come
Looking to purchase
Your virtues.

Beyond Price
Is what they
Take away with them
When they go.

Beyond Price
Is the experience
Of surrendering ourselves
To the Divine
Through Love.

Beyond Price
Is the acceptance
Of the Divine
And living
In that complete embrace.

Beyond Price
Is Your Spiritual Law.

Beyond Price
Is the Court
Where that law
Is practiced.

Beyond Price
Is the Divine Assessment
Where our Purity
Is measured like gold.

Beyond Price
Is that moment when,
By God's Grace,
Our Purity reigns.

Beyond Price
Are the avalanche
Of blessings and gifts
That come to us
At that moment.

Beyond Price
Is being a public sign
Of the sovereignty and dignity
Of the Divine Spirit.

Beyond Price
Are our own actions.

Beyond Price
The Divine Will
Which directs them.

Oh—so far Beyond
Any price
Are these things,
There's no way
To speak of it.

Talking and talking,
We grow tired.

Stay attuned
To the Truth.

Those who recite sacred texts
Talk.

The scholars,
Creating so many descriptions,
Talk.

Brahma talks.
Indra talks.
The devotees of Krishna talk.
Shiva talks.
The intense yogis talk.
So many elders talk.

Desperate souls talk.
Minor gods and goddesses talk.

Saints, ascetic wanderers,
Those who meditate alone,
Those who serve others
Talk.

So many talk.
So many others
Try to talk.

And after all these people
Talk and talk,
They die and die
Going their way.

The Divine made them all.

And the Divine
Will make
So many more.

Those
Who have nothing to say
Are very few.

As great
As You want us to be
Oh Divine Spirit,

That great
You make us.

Nanak knows—
There is only
The One True One.

If someone speaks,
They are misleading
Through words,
And everyone will recognize them
As the fool of all fools.

27

Where is that door,
What is that home
In which You sit
And look after everything?

There are so many
Countless
Subtle melodies
Which call the Creation
Into Being,
Weaving together
In harmony.

How many souls there are
That carry and express
The music.

How many subtle beings
And spirits there are
Who continuously practice
Your Divine Scales.

How many singers there are
Who sing along with Thee.

Air, Water and Fire
Sing to You.

In singing, Thou,
Oh Noble Ruler
Of Spiritual Law
Come to our door.

The beings that record
Our thoughts and deeds
Sing to You,
And, in singing, record
Our actions for all to know.

In this record,
Spiritual Law
Sees clearly
What we are.

The Creative Forces
Of the Universe,
Beautiful and
Always bejeweled,
Sing to You.

The Forces
That govern the Seasons
From the Heavens
Sing to You,

As do the Natural Forces
On the Earth.

The perfected Spiritual Persons
Who ever remain
In Divine Union with Thee
Sing to You.

As do the Disciplined Ones
Who spend their time
In reflection and meditation.

Men and women
Of Moral Self-restraint,
Of Truth
And of Contentment
Sing to You,

As do the Strong
And Noble Heroes.

Learned persons,
Scholars,
And Spiritual masters
Sing to You,

As do
All the Books of Learning
Throughout the ages.

All the enchanting
Visions
Which attract
And enrapture the mind
In the Heavens
On the Earth
And Below
Sing to You.

All the jewels
Created by You
Sing to You,

As do all
The Sacred Places.

The brave and courageous Warriors
Sing to You,

As do the Four Treasures
Of Peace, Contentment,
Love and Divine Union.

All the Universes and Galaxies
Planets in the Solar Systems,
All the Continents
In all the Lands
Sing to You,

And as You continually
Make them,
You protect and support them.

Those who sing to You
Are those who are
Pleasing to You.

They are
Permeated through
With surrendered Love
And become
The Keepers of Thy Essence.

There are so many more
Who sing to You,
I can't even
Think of them all.

Nanak,
How can I even
Talk about it?

Thou, oh Thou
You are always
The True One,
The Master of All.

Truth Pervading.
True Spirit in Form.

You shall ever be—
Though nothing You created
Will go along
With You.

Every color,
Every unique thing
Is continually made
By You.

You who created
All the elements,
And the Divine Cosmic Play
That comes from them,
Creating and creating,
You, Yourself,
Enjoy
What You have done.

And this
Is Your greatness.

You do
What pleases You.

There is nowhere
Your Divine Will
Doesn't prevail.

Oh True Emperor,
Divine King,
Noble of the Noble,

Nanak lives
Surrendered to Your Command.

28

May you wear
The earrings
Of deep contentment.

May humility
Be your begging bowl
And the shawl in which
You carry your belongings.

May being centered
In the center of your being
Be the ashes
That cleanse you.

Wear the patched coat
Of Death.

Keep your body pure,
Like a virgin.

And may the staff
That holds you upright
As you walk along your journey
Be the constant remembrance
Of Spirit within you.

Let the highest
And best company
Be the brotherhood and sisterhood
Of all peoples.

Conquer your mind
To conquer the world.

I bow
To the very act
Of bowing to Thee,
Oh Divine One.

Beyond Time.
Beyond Color.
Beyond Sound.
Beyond Form and Containment.

Age after Age,
You are the One.

29

Nourish yourself
Along your journey
With morsels
Of wisdom.

Let kindness
Bear your burdens
For you,
As the beat of God's Command
Vibrates
In your every
Heartbeat.

Thy, Thyself,
Are the Master.

All else
Follows Thee.

Occult powers
Taste false.

The Great Divine Union,
The Pre-ordained Separation
Both Forces
Run the entire Universe.

I bow
To the very act
Of bowing to Thee,
Oh Divine One.

Beyond Time.
Beyond Color.
Beyond Sound.
Beyond Form and Containment.

Age after Age,
You are the One.

30

There is One Mother
Married
To all time and space.

From Her,
Three Devotees
Are born.

One that creates.
One that nourishes.
One that holds court, deciding the fate.

As it pleases Thee, oh Divine One,
So these devotees move,
Acting according to Thy Divine Command.

The Divine
Sees all.

But the created
Can't see the Divine
At all.

Wow!
This is such
A great drama.

I bow
To the very act
Of bowing to Thee,
Oh Divine One.

Beyond Time.
Beyond Color.
Beyond Sound.
Beyond Form and Containment.

Age after age,
You are the One.

31

You have Your thrones
On every world.

And in every world
You've placed
Your treasures.

Whatever was placed there
By You
Was placed
Once and for all.

Oh Spirit of Union and Connection,
You look out for
All You continually
Make and do.

The True One
Creates
The True Creation.

I bow
To the very act
Of bowing to Thee
Oh Divine One.

Beyond Time.
Beyond Color.
Beyond Sound.
Beyond Form and Containment.

Age after age,
You are the One.

32

If my one tongue
Were to become two,
And the two to become
One million,
And the million
To become 20 million,

Then millions and millions
Of times
I would recite and speak
Of the One Spirit
Pervading and guiding
The Universe.

On this path,
The spouse climbs
With devotion
Step by step
To Union with Thee.

Hearing what is recorded
In the Akashic records,
Even the lowest beings
Have a longing
To return home.

Nanak,
Grace is brought in
As a gift of the Creator.

Those who praise themselves—
False are they
And ever false.

33

The power to speak
Or keep silent—
I don't have that power.

I don't have the power
To beg or to give.

When I live,
When I die—
Is far beyond my power.

I have no power
To rule as a King
With wealth,
Or through the force
Of my own mental manipulations.

I have no power
To attach myself to God through meditation,
Or to attain wisdom,
Or to reflect on what I see.

I have no power
To know the way
To liberate myself
From the world.

Whose Hand
Holds this power?

The One
Who does and sees all.

Nanak,
No one is high
And no one is low.

34

Nights, seasons,
Moon cycles, days.

Wind, water,
Fire and the underworld,

In the midst of this,
The Earth was established
As a place
Where Spirit could evolve
Into a Conscious Awareness of Itself
Protected.

For that purpose,
The souls came
Through time and space
In such a variety
Of colors.

Those souls
Are so many,
They are countless.

There are actions
Upon actions
And we reflect
On what we do.

Thou, oh Divine One,
Are True
And True
Is Your Royal Court
In which all
Is contained.

In Your Royal Court,
Your devotees,
The ones who have found themselves
Within themselves
Look beautiful.

Their actions
Flow from Grace
And this is
The sign of You
They carry.

The Not-Yet-Ripe
And the Ripe
Are both there
On the Earth.

Nanak,
Go and see it.

35

In the Realm of Dharma,
Of Spiritual Law,
We come to understand
How to awaken ourselves
To ourselves.

In the Realm of Wisdom,
We speak
Of how everything
Gets accomplished.

There are so many
Winds, waters and fires.

So many
Creative Forces.

So many
Creations
That the Creator
Is crafting,
Clothing the Spirit
In Form and Color.

So many actions
Done in so many
Lands and places,

So many places
That are not even
Known to us.

All for learning
What You want us
To learn.

So many Heavens,
Moons and Suns.

So many Galaxies
With so many peoples.

So many joined
In Union with Thee.

So many wise ones
And masters.

So many
Robed goddesses.

So many gods
And demons.

So many persons of Honor.

So many jewels of Spiritual instruction
In so many Oceans of Existences.

So many ways
Of thinking about things.

So many words
That come from Thee.

So many rulers
Of Spiritual Nobility.

So many
Living attuned to Thee,
So many of Your servants.

Nanak,
Even Your limits
Are beyond limits.

36

In the Realm of Wisdom,
Wisdom is found.

There,
Beyond Sound,
The subtle
Vibratory frequency
Of creation
Creates the plays
And dramas.

In the Realm of Effort,
The Divine Word
Becomes form.

What is crafted there
Are creations
Of Incomparable Beauty.

It is impossible
To speak
Of these matters.

If someone
Tries to speak,
Afterwards,
He'll only feel mournful
That he couldn't
Describe it.

What is crafted there
Are persons of
Purity, clarity and grace.
Attuned to the Divine
With minds
That know the difference
Between Truth and falsehood,
Persons of genuine understanding
And wisdom.

What is crafted there
Are the psyches
Of angels and masters.

37

In the Realm of Action,
Your Sacred Words
Are power,

And there is no other power
Besides it.

In that Realm
Are brave and strong
Spiritual warriors
Filled
With the presence
Of the Divine.

There,
It is a habit
Sewn securely
Inside them
To honor and praise
Thee.

These beautiful forms
Are impossible
To describe.

The Divine
Dwells
Within their minds.

There,
Those who have
Surrendered themselves
In love to Thee
Live as Lights.

They enjoy
Sweet-tasting bliss
Within themselves.

In the Realm of Truth,
The Formless One dwells.

By seeing All
That is continuously done,
The Divine looks kindly
Upon us and,
In that kind look,
Brings everything
To a state
Of completion.

There are worlds upon worlds,
Solar Systems,
Universes.

If someone tried
To describe them all,
There would be
No limit.

There,
Lights upon Lights
Come into bodies and forms.

And as the Divine Will
Guides them
So they act.

The Divine remains
In a state of contemplation
Seeing and enjoying it all.

Nanak,
Describing this
Forges the hard steel
Of Truth.

38

Let the practice
Of restraining your desires
Be the furnace,

And let calmness
Be the gold-smith.

Let the mind
That knows the difference
Between Truth and falsehood
Be the anvil,

And let what you learn
From your own experience
Be the hammer.

Take your fear
And use it
To stoke the fires
Of your own spiritual discipline,

And let Love
Be the pot
In which the nectar
Of self-awakening,
Of self-awareness
Is poured.

From that,
Fashion the coin
Of speaking
And living
Pure Truth.

Those upon whom
You look kindly,
Oh Divine Spirit,
Act in this way.

Nanak,
The Divine Gaze
Bestows a continuous grace
Which completes
Everything.

Shalok.

The Wind
Is the Guru,
The Teacher,
The Guide,

And Water
Is the Father.

The Mother
Is the great and honored
Earth.

Day and Night
Are the two nurses
In whose lap
The entire world
Plays.

All that is good,
All that is bad,
Are equally embraced
In the presence of the Divine
Under the command of Divine Law.

By your actions,
You, yourself, will know
How close you are to Truth
Or how far away.

Those
Who meditate
In the core
Of their being

Who earn themselves
Through their hard work—

Nanak,
Their faces are radiant and beautiful
And so very many who are connected with them
Are liberated, too.

Who is the Siri Singh Sahib Bhai Sahib Harbhajan Singh Khalsa Yogiji?

In 1969, Harbhajan Singh Khalsa Yogiji (Yogi Bhajan) came to the United States to teach Sikh values and Kundalini Yoga. Through his inspiration, hundreds of thousands of people in the West have heard the teachings of the Sikh Gurus and have embraced the Sikh path.

Who is Ek Ong Kaar Kaur Khalsa?

Ek Ong Kaar Kaur Khalsa is a Western-born woman who, after a long spiritual search, adopted the Sikh path. She is a writer who lives in New Mexico and currently works as the Communications Director for *www.SikhNet.com.*

To order additional copies of Guru Nanak's Japji Sahib: The Song of the Soul visit: www.xlibris.com.

For other books on Kundalini Yoga, Sikh Dharma and the Teachings of Yogi Bhajan, contact:

Ancient Healing Ways
www.a-healing.com
customerservice@a-healing.com

(800) 359-2940 For retail sales
(505) 747-2860 international

(877) 753-5351 For wholesale
(505) 753-5351 international

(505) 747-9718 fax

Ancient Healing Ways
39 Shady Lane
Espanola, NM 87532